Ruby and Louise were practising their magic act
for the Bunny Scouts Talent Show.
But they needed a volunteer.

Ruby and Louise had the same idea. "Max!"

Of course, Max was happy to volunteer.

For the first magic trick, Ruby pulled a coin from Max's ear.

"How?" asked Max.
"A great magician never tells how a trick is done," said Ruby.

For the second magic trick, Louise poured a pitcher full of milk
into a rolled-up newspaper cone. Not one drop of milk dripped out.

Max peeked inside the newspaper cone.
The milk had magically disappeared!

Next, Ruby pulled a yellow handkerchief from her sleeve…
and a blue one…and a green one…and a purple one…
and a red one…and an orange one – with flowers at the end!

"How?" asked Max.
"Magic," whispered Ruby.

Ruby and Louise got ready for the Great Disappearing Trick.
They did not see Max sneak away.

Max found a secret door at the back of the Magic Box.
He had an idea for a trick of his own. He stepped into the box.

Ruby and Louise were now ready for the Great Disappearing Trick.
But their volunteer was gone!
"Maybe Max went into the box," said Louise.

Inside the box, Max heard Ruby and Louise.
He did not want to be found.
What could he do?

Max opened the secret door.
He slipped out the back of the Magic Box.

Max hid behind the box as Ruby came to check inside.

Ruby opened the door. The Magic Box was empty.
"Let's look behind it," said Ruby.

When Ruby closed the front door, Max opened the back door.
He climbed inside the Magic Box again.

Ruby and Louise could not find Max. He had disappeared!
"Now we don't have an audience," said Ruby.

"An audience for what?" asked Grandma, entering the yard.
"Our Great Disappearing Trick!" said Ruby.

"Oh, I love disappearing tricks!" said Grandma.
"How exciting!"
Ruby and Louise began the show.

"Now we will perform the Great Disappearing Trick," said Ruby.
"Before your very eyes, I will make Louise disappear from this Magic Box."
But before Louise could step into the box…

Max reappeared!

"What a wonderful trick!" said Grandma.

"How?" asked Ruby and Louise.

"Magic!" said Max.